The Pride Street Crew

6

Child's Play

Mike Wilson

Published in association with
The Basic Skills Agency

Acknowledgements
Cover: Stuart Williams/The Organisation.
Illustrations: Jim Eldridge.

Orders: please contact Bookpoint Ltd, 39 Milton Park, Abingdon, Oxon OX14 4TD. Telephone: (44) 01235 400414, Fax: (44) 01235 400454. Lines are open from 9.00–6.00, Monday to Saturday, with a 24 hour message answering service. Email address: orders@bookpoint.co.uk

British Library Cataloguing in Publication Data
A catalogue record for this title is available from The British Library

ISBN 0 340 75307 2

First published 1999
Impression number   10 9 8 7 6 5 4 3 2 1
Year   2004 2003 2002 2001 2000 1999

Typeset by Fakenham Photosetting Ltd, Fakenham, Norfolk
Printed in Great Britain for Hodder & Stoughton Educational, a division of Hodder Headline Plc, 338 Euston Road, London NW1 3BH by Athenaeum Press, Gateshead, Tyne & Wear.

JOHN / BONE

WESLEY / TALL

LUKE / SKY

SIMON / CUSTARD

CARL / SPOT

'I love kids,' Lizzy told me.
'I love looking after them.
I want to get a job
looking after kids.

'Do you like kids, Luke?'
she asked.
'Do you think
you will have kids?'

Lizzy was baby-sitting
for Mrs Hill.

Little Jody
was fast asleep upstairs.
There wasn't much
for us to do.

We watched TV
for a bit.
And Lizzy talked
about kids.

Next week is Working Week
at school.
Year 10 go out of school
and work for a week.

I will be working
with my uncle
on the market.

Lizzy has got a job
in a nursery.

'I can't wait,' said Lizzy.

'It will be child's play!' she said.
'And no school
for a week!

'No school skirt.
I can put on what I like!

'No Maths.
No French.

'No stupid little boys.
No stupid little girls.
And no stupid teachers
telling you what to do!'

Next day.

Lizzy got up at 6 o'clock.
Her Mum got up with her.

Mum made tea.
Then it was time to go.

'Good luck,' said Mum.
Mum watched
till Lizzy had gone.

'You'll need it,' she said
with a smile.

Lizzy got to the nursery
in good time.
No children yet.
It was nice and quiet.

Lizzy met a woman
called Raj.
Raj told Lizzy
what to do.

'Don't let them fight.
Don't let them bite you.

'Give them a drink of milk.
But only one biscuit each!

'You look after the sandpit.
But don't let little Jimmy Smith
eat all the sand.'

A woman came in
with a little boy.

'Hello, Mrs West,' said Raj.
'Hello, Tom,' she said
to the little boy.
'And this is Lizzy.
Say hello to Lizzy.'

Tom took one look at Lizzy.
Then he began to cry.

Lizzy tried
to stop him crying.
Raj tried
to stop him crying.
His Mum tried
to stop him crying.
But nobody could stop him.

Tom cried all day,
off and on.

Now and then, he forgot.
But every time
Lizzy went near him,
he started crying again.

At 11 o'clock,
Lizzy made drinks of milk.

Little Jimmy Smith
tipped his drink of milk
in the sandpit.

Mud.

Two little girls
started to laugh.
They did the same.

More mud.

Little Jimmy Smith
picked up the mud
in his hands.
He put it back in his cup.
Then he tried to drink it.

Lizzy got there
just in time.

Then Jimmy got more mud.
He put it in a little girl's hair.
She opened her mouth,
and started to cry.

The mud ran down her face,
and nearly in her mouth.

Lizzy got there
just in time.

Next,
a boy and a girl had a fight
on the fire engine.

Ashot pushed Sam over.
Sam started to cry.

Then Ashot tried
to run her over
with the fire engine.

Lizzy got there
just in time.

Then a little girl called Gemma
tapped Lizzy on the arm.

She looked up at Lizzy
with her pretty little eyes
wide open.

'Please miss,' she said,
'I need a pee-pee.'

Lizzy got there
just in time.

At the end of the day,
Lizzy met me at the market.

'How did it go?' I asked.

'I hate kids!' she said.
'I hate them!'

'I've got sand in my hair,'
Lizzy went on.
'I've got milk in my shoes,
and sick on my new skirt.

'And little Jimmy Smith
bit me on the ear ...'

Lizzy was trying
not to cry.

I put my arm around her.

'But you said
it was child's play,' I said.

'No,' said Lizzy.
'It's not child's play.
It's hard work.
It's too hard!

'I've had it!' she said.

'No more stupid little boys.
No more stupid little girls.
I want to get away
from kids.

'I want to go
back to school!'

If you have enjoyed reading about the Pride Street Crew, you may be interested in other books in the *Livewire* series:

Plays
Beach Babe
A Great Day Out!
Spooky!
Mobile Phoney
Mine Shaft
Sleeping Rough
Clubbing

Chillers
The Cellar
Second Sight
The Rocking Chair
Invisible Ink
Hit and Run
Bargain with a Stranger
The Singer
The Fetch
Life Sentence